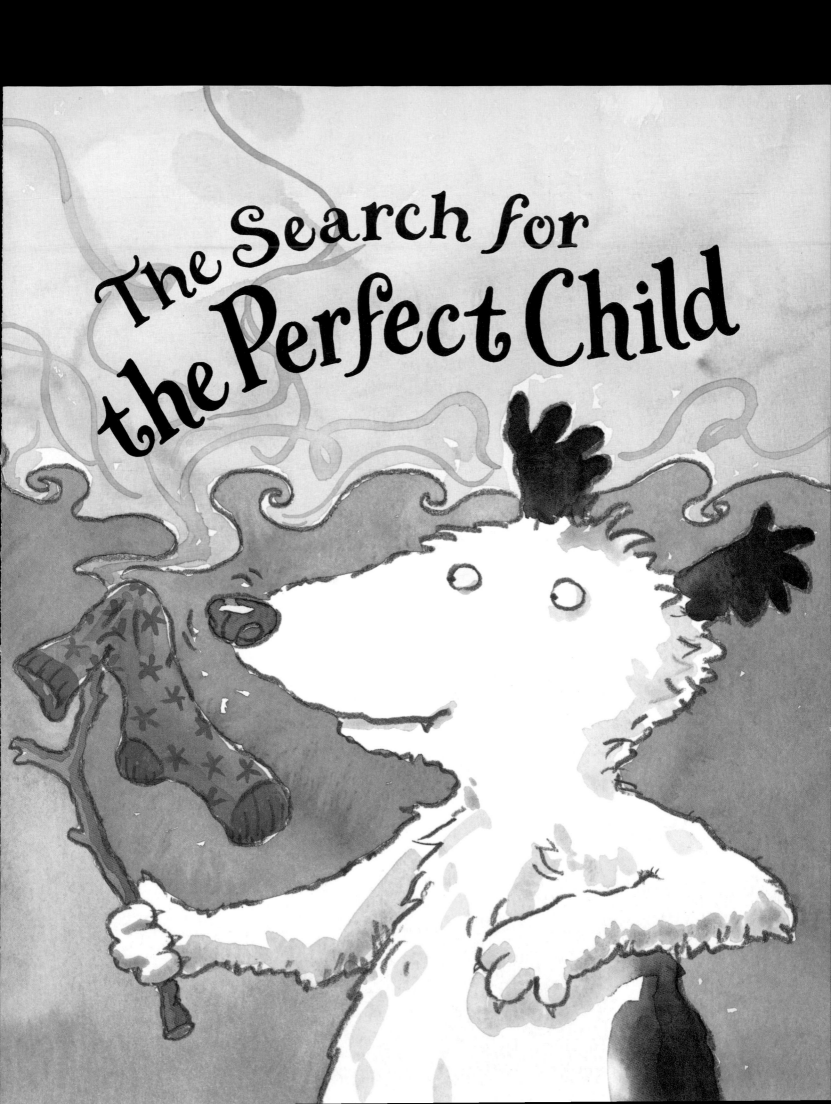

The Search for the Perfect Child

Cookies and thankyous for Denise & Louise

For the cheeky little monkey, aka Zahra

ISBN-13: 978-0-7636-3231-1

ISBN-10: 0-7636-3231-7

Printed in Mexico

This book was typeset in Tapioca.
The illustrations were done in watercolor and ink.

Candlewick Press
2067 Massachusetts Avenue
Cambridge, Massachusetts 02140

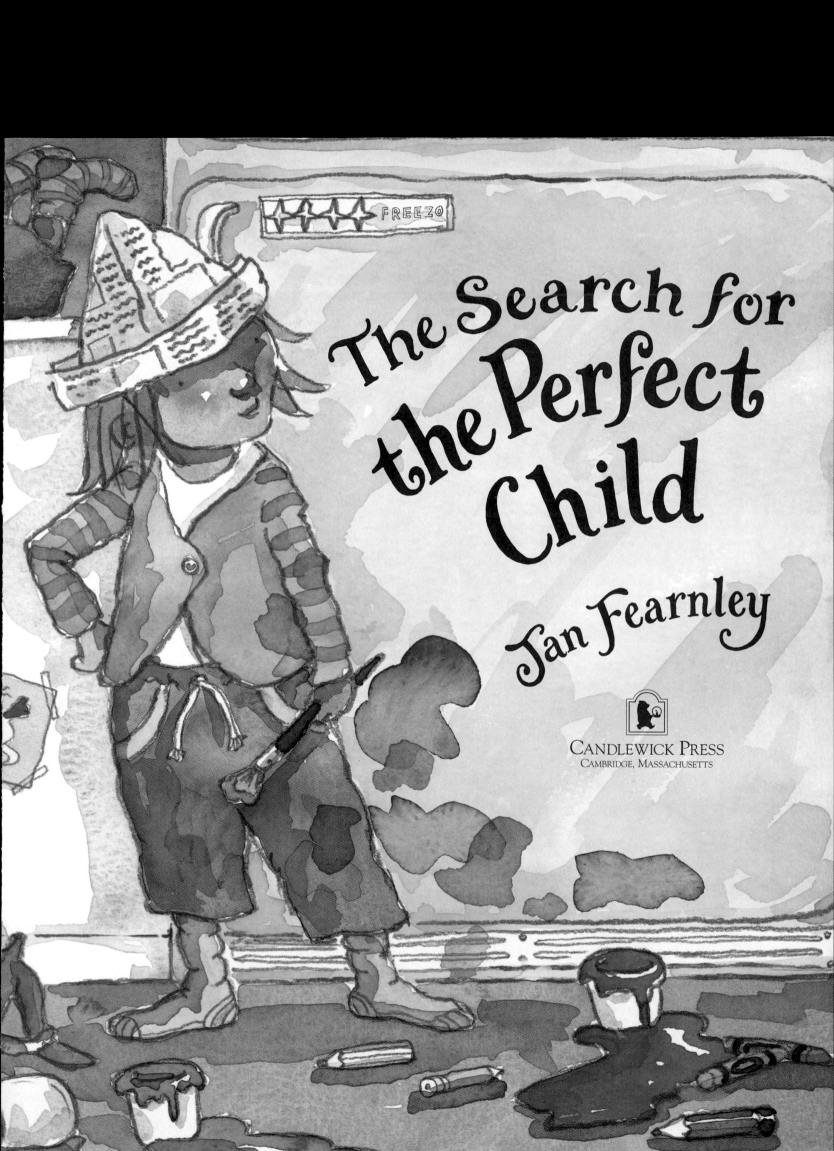

The Search for the Perfect Child

Jan Fearnley

CANDLEWICK PRESS
CAMBRIDGE, MASSACHUSETTS

I'm Fido Farnsworth,
the **cleverest,**
sharpest,
coolest
dog detective in the whole world.

My eyes can spot
anything,
and my nose can sniff out
everything,
even . . .

aliens,

pigs that fly . . .

and gold at the end of the rainbow.

But now I face the hardest job of all—finding the **perfect** child!

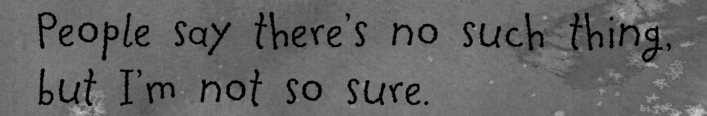

People say there's no such thing,
but I'm not so sure.

Hmmm.

What should I be
looking for?

What makes a
perfect child?

Some people say the
perfect child is creative.

The **perfect** child is kind
to animals . . .

and loves nature.

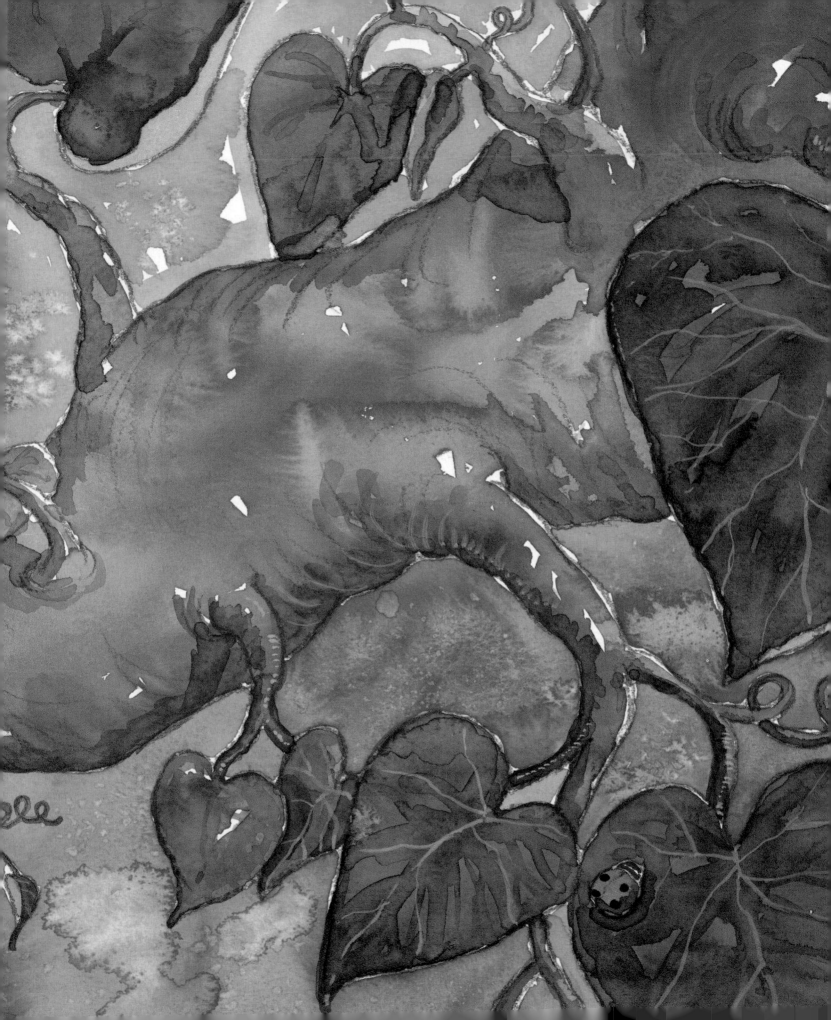

Others say
the **perfect** child has style . . .

and is always happy
to help with the
chores.

The **perfect** child never complains about taking a bath . . .

dinosaurs

playing vampires with friends

underwear jokes

creepy-crawlies

The perfect child
loves to monkey around . . .

and, of course,
is **polite** and **cooperative**
at all times.

Whew! It's not easy finding the **perfect** child.

Have you seen one?

Me too!

I've found you,
and you are
the **perfect** child.